Acting Edition

In Love
and Warcraft

by Madhuri Shekar

ISBN 978-0-573-70325-6

www.concordtheatricals.com
www.concordtheatricals.co.uk

FOR PRODUCTION INQUIRIES

UNITED STATES AND CANADA
info@concordtheatricals.com
1-866-979-0447

UNITED KINGDOM AND EUROPE
licensing@concordtheatricals.co.uk
020-7054-7298

Each title is subject to availability from Concord Theatricals Corp., depending upon country of performance. Please be aware that *IN LOVE AND WARCRAFT* may not be licensed by Concord Theatricals Corp. in your territory. Professional and amateur producers should contact the nearest Concord Theatricals Corp. office or licensing partner to verify availability.

MUSIC AND THIRD-PARTY MATERIALS USE NOTE

IMPORTANT BILLING AND CREDIT REQUIREMENTS

IN LOVE AND WARCRAFT was first produced by the Alliance Theatre in Atlanta, Georgia in 2014. The performance was directed by Laura Kepley, with sets by Andrew Boyce, lighting by Liz Lee, sound by Kendall Simpson, and costumes by Lex Liang. The Production Stage Manager was R. Lamar Williams, and the Dramaturg was Celise Kalke. The cast was as follows:

EVIE..Lily Balsen

KITTY... Alexandra Ficken

RAUL.. Evan Cleaver

RYAN.. Patrick Halley

MALE..Bobby Labartino

FEMALE.......................................Diany Rodriguez

CHARACTERS

EVIE – a 22-year-old college senior
KITTY – 22, Evie's best friend
RAUL – 25, One of Evie's clients
RYAN – 25, Evie's somewhat boyfriend

Some of the miscellaneous characters
(ideally played by one male and female actor):

Male:

TONY – a gamer, **JERRY** – a Lakers fan
NATHAN – Evie's hairdresser, **MAN** – a man in a movie theatre
MONSTER – a Warcraft monster

Female:

CHAI – a gamer, and Tony's aggrieved girlfriend,
CHARLOTTE – Evie's client, **WOMAN** – a woman in a movie theatre
DOCTOR – Evie's OB/GYN

SETTING

A college campus in Southern California
Evie's apartment
Raul's apartment
A doctor's office
A bar
Inside Warcraft Universe

TIME

Present Day

WARCRAFT GLOSSARY

Avatar – A graphical representation of the player's character.

Battle Rez – A resurrection spell cast while in combat to bring a player or group back to life.

Boss – The monster

Cosplay – Costume Play- dressing up and performing as specific characters or ideas.

Damage Dealers – Players responsible for inflicting damage in the group.

Debuffs – A spell or ability that decreases a players effectiveness, usually cast by in-game enemies.

DPS/Deeps – Damage Per Second- a measure of the damage inflicted by a person or group.

End Game – the part of the game where level advancement is no longer the goal.

Guild – An in-game association of players. A team.

Healer – Spellcasters with the power to heal other players.

iLevel – Item Level. A measure of how powerful a players gear is.

IRL – In real life

L2P! – Learn to play!

Mage food – magically conjured food to nourish the player

N00bs – Newbies (new players)

Ready Check – checking to see if all the players are ready to proceed

Slash or Forward Slash – the "/" key typed before each gaming command

Strats – Strategies

Tank – The player in the group assigned to absorb the damage

Twenty-five manning – Running a raid dungeon designed for a group of 25 players.

Vial of Sands – An item that can let you transform into a transport animal

Wipe – A wipeout- where the entire party or raid is killed.

BABY PLEASE

(EVIE, 22, stands by herself on stage. She wears a hoodie, jeans, and a pair of gaming headphones with a mic. She looks out, and starts to speak. Heartfelt.)

EVIE. Baby please. Just hear me out. I know I screwed up, okay? I know I'm an asshole. But I – I love you. Beyond anything I can control, I love you, Chai. I know I don't deserve it – I know – but if you could find it in your heart to forgive me …

(Suddenly matter-of-fact. Into her mic.)

Tony, are you writing this down?

(Lights change. EVIE is not by herself. She has her laptop set up on a table in her apartment. In two other spaces (not in her apartment) RYAN, 25, and TONY, 19, play on their own laptops, gaming headphones in place.)

(There is another workstation with a laptop set up, but no one is sitting there.)

TONY. Got it. I screwed up. I'm an asshole. Please forgive me. My spicy Chai latte.

EVIE. Do NOT call her your spicy chai latte.

(They're all typing and clicking, fast and furious, deeply immersed in the game.)

RYAN. We don't have the deeps for the raid. I'm blowing all my CDs just clearing trash.

TONY. Evie, I know you do this for a living, but I know my Chai.

EVIE. Yeah, and now you know her roommate even better.

TONY. Hey –

EVIE. Rule number one of Warcraft, Tony. Never stand in the fire.

TONY. *(overlapping)* Never stand in the fire. I know.

EVIE. If you knew you were attracted to her roommate, you shoulda just stayed away.

But no, you had to be a dumbass.

RYAN. Our hit points are dropping!

EVIE. And because of you, she's not logging on, we're one man down for the raid –

TONY. She'll log on, okay. She's mad at me, she's not gonna punish the guild.

RYAN.	**EVIE.**
Yeah, right.	Yeah, right.

(CHAI, 19, pissed off, enters and takes her place at the fourth laptop. She puts on her gaming headphones.)

(The others gasp in relief.)

TONY. Chai, you're online!

CHAI. I'm not talking to you, Moldrok. Azareth, Dragnathor, what's our status?

(Everyone is typing furiously. The team is complete.)

RYAN. Okay, trash is pretty much cleared, but we're totally out of pots, and the boss is in the shadows.

EVIE. Ready check passed, pulling boss in 3 – 2 – 1...

TONY. *(awkwardly, while playing)* Baby, Chai, look I know you're mad – I screwed up, I – HEY WHAT THE HELL –

CHAI. Ouch, Moldrok, looks like you took a pretty bad hit.

TONY. Look, I'm sorry, okay, I'm sorry, I really am –

EVIE. Chai, I'm not able to access the emergency vault – what are you doing?

RYAN. Fuck, I can't get into the vault either.

TONY. Baby don't do this. This is a mistake.

CHAI. Oh you're telling me what to do now, buttface?

EVIE. Moldrok! Tony! Don't stand in the fire! Don't stand in the fucking fire!

TONY. AAAAAH!

RYAN. Fuck! Great. Moldrok's down. He's dead.

(EVIE *picks up her phone and starts dialing.*)

TONY. What? Chai! Heal me!

CHAI. *(pounding her keyboard)* Why don't you ask Brenda to heal you, bitch?

TONY. Are you literally kicking me when I'm dead?

(TONY*'s phone rings and he picks up.*)

What?

EVIE. *(on the phone)* Go to her dorm.

TONY. What?

EVIE. Go to her dorm. Right now. Tell her the speech I wrote for you. Word for word.

TONY. I don't remember.

EVIE. Bluetooth it. BLUETOOTH. NOW.

(TONY *wears a Bluetooth device and runs out of his room.*)

RYAN. Battle rezzing Moldrok, boss going into phase 2 in 3 – 2 – CHAI WHAT THE HELL ARE YOU DOING!?

CHAI. You know what, this game is stupid.

(RYAN *gasps.*)

EVIE. *(struggling to stay calm)* Chai, I know you're hurting, but we don't have to sink to that level.

(TONY *bursts into* CHAI*'s room.* CHAI *looks at him in astonishment.*)

TONY. Chai, baby. Please. Just … hear me out. I … I …

CHAI. What?

(EVIE *talks into her phone, connected to* TONY*'s Bluetooth.*)

EVIE. I screwed up.

TONY. I screwed up.

EVIE. I did the one thing I swore I would never do, I hurt you.

TONY. I did the one thing I swore I would never do, I hurt you.

EVIE. But I love you. More than anything else in the world.

TONY. But I love you. More than anything else in the world.

EVIE. I can't live without you Chai. You're my better half.

TONY. I can't live without you Chai. You're my better half.

EVIE. You have been for three semesters and 600 hours of gameplay, that has mean something, right?

(RYAN stops typing.)

RYAN. What?

EVIE. Not you, sweetie. Keep playing.

TONY. *(finishing)* … That has to mean something, right?

(The moment of truth. CHAI is moved, but not completely.)

(TONY is lost. EVIE blurts –)

EVIE. Spicy chai latte! SPICY CHAI LATTE!

TONY. Please take me back! My spicy Chai latte.

(CHAI melts.)

CHAI. Oh Tony. I hate you.

(They start making out furiously. EVIE listens in.)

EVIE. Okay! I think it worked.

(TONY and CHAI, still making out, disappear from view – they're no longer playing the game.)

EVIE. Moldrok. Tony? Chai?

RYAN. Where the fuck are they?

EVIE. … I think we just lost them.

RYAN. WHAT? WE LOST OUR DPS? What are they doing???

(EVIE's back on the game. Fast and furious.)

EVIE. Having sex, probably.

RYAN. FUCKERS.

EVIE. Yeah, exactly.

RYAN. Why the hell would they be having sex when we're on the verge of a legendary server first boss kill? I mean what the hell is wrong with them?

EVIE. They just don't get it. What can I say? Let's focus. We can do this.

RYAN. We are two men down. There is no fucking way we can do this.

EVIE. FOLLOW MY LEAD. You have to be our DPS and healer – I'm taking the damage –

RYAN. That's a wipe, run back!

EVIE. Ryan, Ryan. Listen. I'm almost there.

RYAN. What?

EVIE. Just – let me – there – take that! And that! And that!

RYAN. Oh my god. That's so good. Keep doing that.

EVIE. Are you feeling me baby?

RYAN. Right there.

EVIE. Aaaaargh!

RYAN. DO IT!

EVIE. NUKE IT! FOCUS FIRE!

RYAN. FEEL THE POWER!

EVIE. AND THAT!

(Pause. Breathing heavily.)

And that's it. It's dead.

(They both lie back in their chairs, panting.)

RYAN. That was great. You were great.

EVIE. So were you.

RYAN. You were better.

EVIE. Yeah. I was.

*(**KITTY**, **EVIE**'s best friend and roommate, walks into the apartment. Little black dress, sex hair, and carrying her spiky stilettos in her hand.)*

(She looks at EVIE *at the computer, still panting.)*

KITTY. What kinda porn you watching?

EVIE. Kitty. *(into the mic:)* Hey, BRB.

KITTY. Look at you, all flushed and sexy. You sure I didn't interrupt anything?

EVIE. Where have you been?

*(*KITTY *walks about the place, dropping her possessions wherever she pleases, effortlessly creating a mess.)*

KITTY. I told you, I had a date with Mason.

EVIE. Yeah, on Tuesday, like 48 hours ago.

KITTY. It was a good date. I have to get rid of him.

EVIE. What?

KITTY. I hate having a boyfriend. I hate being exclusive. He's a fucking weirdo.

EVIE. Why?

*(*KITTY *perches on the edge of the couch.)*

KITTY. He said his mother's name in bed this morning.

*(*RYAN *laughs, overhearing.)*

RYAN. Hehehe. Nice.

EVIE. *(into her mic)* Dragnathor, I'm taking 5.

(She takes off her headphones. When she does, RYAN *disappears.* EVIE *turns to* KITTY, *concerned.)*

Are you sure?

KITTY. He said "MEREDITH" when he came.

(She flops backwards onto the couch.)

KITTY. I can't do this anymore. This is just like, the last straw.

EVIE. Then break up with him already. I don't even know what you guys have in common besides sex.

KITTY. What else do you need?

(pause)

I need to make him break up with me, though. I can't be the bitch who dumped him. We're in the same study group.

(pause)

How do I do this?

(EVIE starts turning back to her computer.)

EVIE. Kitty. I help couples stay together. I don't help them break up.

(KITTY grabs her.)

KITTY. Save me, I'm dying here.

EVIE. *(thinking)* The answer's pretty obvious when you think about it.

(pause)

Stop having sex with him. Tell him... he's not doing it for you anymore.

(KITTY lets go.)

KITTY. Ouch.

EVIE. Withhold sex long enough, and he'll break up with you. But his pride will stop him from telling people why.

KITTY. *(pause)* Of course your solution is to cut off sex all together.

(EVIE goes back to her computer.)

EVIE. Life is a lot less complicated without it. You'll see.

(She starts typing.)

(KITTY looks at her, affectionate, sad. KITTY kisses her on the neck.)

EVIE. Ew, stop it.

KITTY. What are you doing tonight? Let's go out and get you laid.

EVIE. *(suddenly remembering)* No thanks. I'm meeting with a new client.

KITTY. Ugh, you are the worst.

EVIE. *(looking at her watch)* Oh, shit, I'm meeting with a new client on the quad. Like, five minutes ago.

(KITTY saunters off. EVIE puts on her headphones. RYAN appears.)

I have to go.

RYAN. WHAT? You can't! The monster's coming back to life! I need you!

EVIE. I'm late for the meeting with the new client. Remember? I told you about him.

RYAN. Blow him off, dude! Who cares about your stupid clients? This is important!

EVIE. I'm sorry, you have to manage solo for a little bit. Slash kiss!

(She shuts down her laptop, grabs her bag, and runs out of her apartment.)

RYAN. EVIE! EVELYN! THIS IS SO NOT COOL!

(pause)

Fucking. Fuck. Great. I'm decapitated. I don't have my head. I am lacking a head. Which is like, the most important organ. I hope you're happy.

(He looks around. He's by himself. He takes a sip of his beer.)

IT WOULD BE NICE IF THERE WAS MORE

(Outside the campus cafe, in the quad. EVIE rushes in, cradling her laptop in her hand – still playing.)

(RAUL, 22, very easy on the eyes, sits with a cup of coffee and notices EVIE.)

EVIE. *(into her headset)* Let me take care of the fireballs – get out of the way – just try and find your head!

(She bangs into RAUL.)

Shit! Sorry!

RAUL. No problem.

(She turns around and sees RAUL.)

(She is struck speechless.)

Are you okay?

(We hear the aggravated squeaks of RYAN from her headset.)

Are you okay?

EVIE. Yes. Sorry.

RAUL. Are you Evie?

(EVIE shuts down the laptop.)

EVIE. Y – yes – are you my – Raul – my client – sorry – Raul?

RAUL. That's me.

EVIE. You... have the girlfriend problem. You have a girlfriend! Great!

RAUL. Um –

(She sits down at his table.)

EVIE. I'm so sorry I'm late – I just lost track of time –

RAUL. It's fine. What were you –

EVIE. Oh, it's just Warcraft Universe. You know, like World of Warcraft?

RAUL. Oh. Cool.

EVIE. *(putting away her stuff)* Yeah. Anyway –

RAUL. I didn't think girls played that.

EVIE. Some do.

RAUL. That's pretty cool.

EVIE. *(sudden enthusiasm)* It is!

> *(a second...)*

> It's really cool.

RAUL. *(amused)* Cool.

> *(an awkward moment)*

RAUL. So... I need to tell you something.

EVIE. *(back to business)* Right, right. Your email said you needed a letter for your girlfriend?

RAUL. Ex-girlfriend.

EVIE. What?

RAUL. That's the thing. We broke up. This afternoon.

EVIE. Shit. I'm... so sorry.

RAUL. So... to be honest... I'm not really sure why I came.

EVIE. Well you want her back, right?

RAUL. Can you do that?

EVIE. Yeah.

RAUL. Really. You sound pretty confident.

EVIE. I'm good at this.

RAUL. I've heard.

> *(leaning forward)*

> You write love letters, right? That's what you do?

EVIE. Well, whatever people need. Love letters, emails, text messages, Facebook wall posts, telegrams...

RAUL. Telegrams?

EVIE. Oh yeah. "Baby. Stop. I screwed up. Stop. Take me back. Stop." It's not rocket science really.

> *(RAUL smiles.)*

> I do some hidden microphone work sometimes. Feed you lines when you're with your girlfriend.

RAUL. That's wild. And it always works?

EVIE. Relationships aren't as complicated as people think. All you need are the right words. The right commands, the right strategies.

RAUL. Like a game.

EVIE. Yeah, pretty much.

RAUL. That's kind of cynical. What about love?

EVIE. What about it?

RAUL. Isn't that what's important? Can you really make someone love you with just the right commands, the right strategies?

EVIE. I... look – if you don't want –

RAUL. Sorry. I'm just a little curious, I guess. About you.

EVIE. *(automatically)* Why? *(flustered)* I mean, we're here to help you, right? Help you get back with your girlfriend.

RAUL. *(pause)* Yeah.

EVIE. Okay. Let's do it.

(She takes out her notebook and pen.)

What's her name?

RAUL. Monica.

EVIE. And why did you break up?

RAUL. We... we fight a lot. She... she gets angry. A lot.

EVIE. Why?

RAUL. I don't know... My friends say she's crazy. But – she – she just. I'm never good enough, you know? I keep trying to make her happy, but I'm just... tired of it. I can't always be there for her. And even if I like, look at another girl, she totally freaks out.

EVIE. Why did you break up today?

RAUL. I didn't reply to a text.

(He laughs.)

Kinda dumb, right? She texted me last night, nothing important you know, and I was out, I didn't reply, and today she exploded. And I just... left.

(pause)

And I feel bad, I guess. I feel bad. I just want to make this work.

EVIE. Do you love her?

RAUL. I mean, yeah. We've been together two years.

EVIE. Okay. Well, like you said, love is important.

(She crooks a smile. He looks at her. She looks away.)

EVIE. Okay.

(pause, preparing to write)

She's… insecure. Sounds like. That's why she's jealous. Does she have any reason to be?

RAUL. What do you mean?

EVIE. You know.

RAUL. Okay, look. We broke up a lot, okay? And sometimes when we were broken up, I'd… see… other people, but I never technically cheated on her. I'm not a cheat.

EVIE. No judgement here, Daddy-o, I've seen a lot worse.

RAUL. Daddy-o?

EVIE. Ignore that. So what made you get back together each time?

RAUL. *(impish)* Well, getting back together after a huge fight… well… I mean… it was pretty… pretty fucking amazing, you know?

EVIE. *(She doesn't.)* Sure.

RAUL. But…

(He drifts off, thoughtful.)

(She clears her throat.)

(He returns, and looks at her, almost startled.)

It would be nice if there was more.

(They look at each other. **EVIE** *holds his gaze this time, tapping into her nerve reserve.)*

I know what I want, and I want to feel that. I can't put it into words, but – I know what it is. It's deep, you know? It's more than what we have right now. Yeah, the sex is great, but it's… hunger. It's… wanting. It's…

(beat)

Do you… know what I mean?

EVIE. Yeah.

(She starts writing, thinking out loud.)

Dear Monica.

(pause)

How can I put into words, the pain that I feel when you're not with me? It is not something that language was made for. This pain is so deep, in my bones, in my blood, so deep inside me that it has no beginning and no end. I wake up at night in a cold sweat, because you are not by my side.

(pause, embarrassed)

Shit.

RAUL. What?

EVIE. Sorry. Let's try again –

RAUL. No, that's... That's beautiful. Can I –

*(He leans over to look at her pad, to see what she's written. He's very close. **EVIE** can't take it. He looks at her.)*

Go on.

EVIE. *(mouth dry)* Your every touch fills me with a rush of joy, so powerful, my whole being quivers, waiting for you, wanting you...

(His hand brushes hers. She nearly jumps out of her seat.)

RAUL. Sorry.

EVIE. Sorry.

RAUL. Sorry.

(Pause. He looks at her pad.)

Your handwriting's... cute.

EVIE. My handwriting?

RAUL. Do you really feel that much... when you're in love?

EVIE. I don't know.

RAUL. You don't know?

EVIE. I don't do… that.

RAUL. You don't do love?

EVIE. Sure, I –

(pause, nervously laughing)

What does that even mean?

*(**RAUL** looks at her. She ducks her head and quickly writes a few more lines on her pad. She tears off the page and gives it to him.)*

Here. She'll take you back.

RAUL. Uh –

EVIE. Good luck.

(She quickly grabs her things and leaves, not looking back.)

TRANSITION: SELFIE

(A guy and a girl walk across stage. The girl is trying hard to take a selfie of the two of them, and is failing. The guy hurries ahead.)

CLAIRE. Hold up! Rodney, hold up!

(She catches up with him and they try again.)

Angle, Rodney, angle your face!

RODNEY. Claire. We're late for class.

CLAIRE. We can't be Facebook official if you can't even take a decent selfie! Now smile!

*(Click. Fail. **RODNEY** keeps moving, he's late.)*

*(**CLAIRE** looks at her phone, frustrated.)*

Why the fuck are you so tall?!

(OR)

Ugh, I look gross. Rodney!

(She follows him out.)

UGLY WOMEN GET LAID ALL THE TIME

(**EVIE** *is on her laptop outside the cafe. She has her headset on.*)

EVIE. *(into her mic)* Stop poking the troll, Dragnathor, what did he ever do to you?

(pause)

Come on, this is supposed to be like our relaxing date. Away from the battle.

(Pause. She stops typing.)

Hey, Ryan.

Do you wanna… Do you wanna meet IRL this weekend? Yes, in real life. We could like… hang out? Cosplay? Or something. I don't know.

(**KITTY** *enters and goes up to her.*)

KITTY. Well, it happened.

(**EVIE** *looks up.*)

EVIE. What?

KITTY. It happened!

EVIE. Oh, just a second.

(into her headset)

Hey Dragnathor, need to hearth out from the Mermaid Lagoon for a few minutes, got an IRL thing, BRB. Keep farming that leather.

(She powers down.)

Hey, what's up?

KITTY. What the fuck are you talking about?

EVIE. I'm on a date with Ryan.

KITTY. Is he… here?

EVIE. No, he's home in San Diego.

KITTY. How can you be on a date if you're not even in the same place?

EVIE. Oh, we are.

(pause)

We were just exploring the Mermaid Lagoon. It's beautiful. You should come sometime.

KITTY. I'd rather come for real.

EVIE. Kitty.

KITTY. Anyway. It happened. He broke up with me.

EVIE. Wow. Already?

KITTY. It was so hard…

EVIE. Should I ask?

KITTY. The holding out. It was difficult. It was agony.

EVIE. How long did it take?

KITTY. 22 hours.

EVIE. No sex for 22 hours and he dumps you?

KITTY. I don't blame him! If he pulled the same shit on me I'd be done with him in 20 minutes!

EVIE. Well. Good then. This is what you wanted, right?

KITTY. *(as a question)* Yeah.

EVIE. Great. You're welcome. Hey. That advice was on the house. Special BFF discount.

KITTY. You are such a dork.

EVIE. *(dorky)* And I own it!

(into her headset)

Hey babe. No, she's still here.

(to KITTY*)*

He says hi.

KITTY. Hi, Ryan. Dragnathor. Whatever.

EVIE. *(into the headset)* Yup, still powered down. Maybe you can get another beer or something.

KITTY. When are you gonna dump him?

*(*EVIE *unplugs her headset.)*

EVIE. Kitty! He could have heard you!

KITTY. I know.

EVIE. Why should I dump him?

KITTY. Because he's a loser.

EVIE. Gamers are not losers, okay? Do you think I'm a loser?

KITTY. Of course not! That's the whole point! You're not a loser! You shouldn't be dating a loser!

EVIE. He's not a loser. He's just… trying to find himself.

KITTY. He's 25. He doesn't have a job. He lives in his parents' basement. He uses your money to buy TOYS.

EVIE. Uh – collectibles.

KITTY. TOYS! My God! Evie! He's not even that cute! What do you see in him!

EVIE. He gets me, okay? It's comfortable.

KITTY. And they lived comfortably ever after.

EVIE. What's so horrible about that?

KITTY. I don't get you. You spend so much time fixing other people's relationships and you can't even see what's broken about yours.

EVIE. Broken?

KITTY. Just because you're so freaking scared of sex doesn't mean you have to load yourself down with a guy no one would ever wanna fuck!

EVIE. You're not yourself today.

KITTY. What do you think? I just got dumped.

EVIE. Oh, Kitty. I'm sorry.

(EVIE *reaches out and* KITTY *scoots over.* EVIE *hugs her.*)

KITTY. It's just… a change. You know? It's a… shock. To the system. I haven't ever gone this long without getting any.

EVIE. 22 hours?

KITTY. Well, at least it's not 22 years.

(EVIE *pushes her away playfully.*)

EVIE. (*plugging in her headset*) Hey, babe? Um. Gonna have to take a raincheck on our date. Yeah, sorry.

KITTY. Hey, no, it's fine.

EVIE. *(mouthing "It's okay")* Uh, before that – what do you think? About what we were talking about? Wanna come up to L.A. tomorrow? I'm free.

(She listens.)

No, it's okay. I understand. Yeah. Totally. No, you go ahead. I'll catch up with you later.

(She slides her headset off, it hangs around her neck.)

KITTY. What's his excuse?

EVIE. His dad won't let him borrow the car.

(pause)

That's legit, right?

(KITTY raises an eyebrow.)

KITTY. You could do so much better, Evie. To start with, if you just cleaned yourself up a little bit, you'd be kinda cute.

EVIE. Thank you?

KITTY. You should go to Nathan!

EVIE. No.

KITTY. Come on, he loves you.

EVIE. He talks too much.

KITTY. I'll make an appointment.

EVIE. Even if I clean myself up, I'll still look like me, so what's the point.

KITTY. You're actually pretty, Evelyn. And you just don't see it.

EVIE. I know who I am, and –

KITTY. And even. Even! If you weren't pretty, okay? That doesn't matter. Ugly women get laid all the time! Haven't you ever been to Walmart? Ugly people making out! Everywhere!

(pause)

It's kinda sweet.

EVIE. Ahhh.

(EVIE looks past her. RAUL has just walked in. RAUL looks at EVIE and smiles. He goes in to the cafe to get a drink.)

KITTY. What?

(looks around, spots RAUL)

Who. Is. That.

EVIE. Just a client.

KITTY. Hellooooo daddy. Well, isn't his timing perfect.

(She adjusts her cleavage.)

EVIE. Not him.

KITTY. Why not?

EVIE. He – uh – he… has a girlfriend.

KITTY. *(knowingly)* Oh, really. Is that all?

EVIE. Yeah. What else could there be?

KITTY. Mm-hmm. And do you hate that girlfriend?

EVIE. Of course not. They were broken up, and I helped him get back together with her.

(KITTY smacks EVIE's arm in frustration.)

EVIE. Ow!

KITTY. Dammit Evie! This is what I'm talking about! A specimen of pure gorgeousness admits that he's single, and you help him get back together with his ex-girlfriend? What is wrong with you?

EVIE. Calm down, he's coming over.

KITTY. What?

EVIE. Shh. He's coming over. Shit. He's walking. He's walking. He's here. Oh God.

(He's there.)

RAUL. Hey.

EVIE. Hello. Greetings.

RAUL. You look good.

EVIE. Haha. *(They stare at each other for a second. KITTY extends her hand.)*

KITTY. Hi, I'm Kitty.

EVIE. Oh, sorry. Raul, this is my roommate Kitty. Kitty, Raul.

RAUL. Hey.

KITTY. You look familiar. Have we met?

EVIE. *(warning)* Kitty…

KITTY. No, really, I'm actually asking like seriously.

RAUL. Maybe. It's a big campus.

KITTY. Hmm.

EVIE. Yep.

RAUL. Sorry, didn't mean to interrupt.

KITTY. Oh, no interrupting. I was just… going… to… yoga. At…the… yoga place. So I should. Get… going… to… yoga.

    (pause)

You kids have fun.

EVIE. Bye, Kitty.

RAUL. Nice meeting you.

KITTY. Pleasure.

    *(**RAUL** sits down. When his back is turned, **KITTY** makes a pretty obvious "fuck him" gesture. **EVIE** motions for her to get lost. **KITTY** winks and exits.)*

RAUL. Did you change your hair?

EVIE. Uh, I washed it?

RAUL. It looks good.

EVIE. Yay. Hygiene: 1. Hair: 0.

    *(**EVIE** fidgets.)*

RAUL. You, uh, you kind of ran off the other day –

EVIE. Oh, yes, I just – you know. Busy busy. Chop chop. Stuff.

RAUL. What you wrote for me – it was… pretty amazing.

EVIE. Oh, I – thank you. Thanks.

RAUL. I've just never really heard it put that way. Never really felt it, you know?

EVIE. So… did it work? Did she take you back?

RAUL. I wouldn't know. I never gave it to her.

EVIE. Why not?

RAUL. Because none of it was true.

EVIE. I thought you liked it.

RAUL. I loved it. I just… I realized I didn't want it with her.

EVIE. I – I'm sorry, if… I… I didn't mean to imply that – you guys weren't –

RAUL. No. You were right.

(pause)

I just wish I'd realized sooner, you know?

(pause)

Like, I'd met you sooner.

EVIE. Okay.

(She laughs nervously.)

(pause)

RAUL. Anyway. Um. I believe I owe you…

(He reaches for his wallet –)

EVIE. Oh, no, keep it.

RAUL. But I haven't paid yet –

EVIE. No, don't worry about it. Seriously. I – uh. You're single again. I didn't exactly follow through on my guarantee.

RAUL. Well then, maybe you can help me out with that.

EVIE. Sure!

RAUL. Will you have dinner with me, Evie?

EVIE. Excuse me?

RAUL. Do you wanna have dinner some time?

(pause)

Tonight? Tomorrow. Sunday. Monday.

(pause)

Lunch? Coffee? A quick conversation as we pass each other on the street?

EVIE. You're asking me out.

RAUL. I am.

EVIE. On a date.

RAUL. I'm trying to, yes.

EVIE. Ho. Wow.

(pause)

I don't know what to say.

RAUL. It's usually a yes-or-no kinda deal.

EVIE. Wow. Um. You see the thing is… there's someone. I mean.

RAUL. I'm sorry. I just – thought. You're seeing someone?

EVIE. Not in real life.

RAUL. What does that mean?

EVIE. Nothing.

RAUL. So you're not seeing someone.

EVIE. No, I'm not… *not* seeing someone.

(tiny pause)

Let's do it.

RAUL. Great. When are you free?

EVIE. Tomorrow night?

RAUL. Let's get dinner?

EVIE. Great.

RAUL. Great. I'll text you.

EVIE. Great!

(He smiles at her and leaves. EVIE lets out a long breath.)

(She goes back to her computer, and puts on her headset.)

(She realizes it's been on the whole time.)

Shit. Shit. Ryan! Ryan? Are you there? Are you still there? Did you –

(Lights up on **RYAN***. In his room. Wearing his headset. He's heard the whole thing. He turns it off, angrily.)*

Ryan?

(pause)

Phew. That was close.

STRAIGHT GUYS. DON'T FUCK 'EM

(EVIE *sits in a salon chair as* NATHAN *styles her hair.*)

NATHAN. And it was only when he took off my blindfold that I realized he wasn't circumcised. And this – believe it or not – first time I've seen a turtleneck in real life. I wasn't expecting it, okay, you can't blame me. It looked like… like… like that pokemon that turns into a bug, but it's still in a cocoon. Anyway. So I get over it and we're fooling around, and just when I have his balls in my mouth, there's this terrific BANG on the door. It was his crazy puta roommate, just screaming at him to open the door. So he hobbles over to the door and tries to calm her down, feeding her some bullshit about dying of the flu or some shit, and how he needs to be alone. Anyway he gets back on the bed and rolls over and then HE starts screaming. "You're bleeding, you're bleeding!" I look down and I got blood all over me. And then I realize hey it's not me – HIS dick is bleeding. Like gushing. And first I was like shit, did I just bite off one of his nuts or what? He started going loco, freaking the fuck out. Then finally the truth came out! Turns out like a month ago he got his dick caught in his zipper, and tore it when he tried to get it out. The doc told him to get stitches but he never did. Dios mio, I was washing blood off me all weekend.

(EVIE *sits still, helpless.*)

(NATHAN *looks at her in the mirror and laughs.*)

You look so traumatized.

EVIE. What was up with the roommate?

NATHAN. Turns out she was his wife.

EVIE. Oh, no.

NATHAN. Straight guys. Don't fuck 'em. Not worth it.

EVIE. I'm way ahead of you there.

NATHAN. So how was YOUR weekend?

EVIE. Oh, not nearly as exciting.

NATHAN. Yeah, why's that? You still scared of dick?

EVIE. Nathan. Do you have to be so crude?

NATHAN. Well pardon me, Miss Manners. I meant, are you still afeared of the male member?

EVIE. You tell me stories like that, what do you expect?

(He spins her around in the swivel chair.)

NATHAN. Okay, let's do your face.

(He starts applying makeup.)

NATHAN. So who's the hot date tonight?

EVIE. What makes you think I'm going on a date?

NATHAN. Oh, please. Look at you. You're blushing.

EVIE. I am not.

NATHAN. *(sing-song)* Evie has a crush.

EVIE. Shut up.

NATHAN. *(sing-song)* Somebody's gonna get lucky.

EVIE. Not gonna be me.

NATHAN. Why not?

EVIE. Because.

NATHAN. Then why are you going out with him?

EVIE. I don't know. He asked me.

NATHAN. Mm-hmm.

EVIE. That's it. It's probably… I mean… It's just probably just gonna be a one-off thing, you know. He's gonna shake my hand like a gentleman and tell me that I was very pleasant company, and that maybe we'll see each other around sometime.

NATHAN. Stop, or I'm gonna puke on your face.

EVIE. Please don't.

NATHAN. Come on, get a little more excited. You got a hot date tonight. You gotta pull out all the stops.

EVIE. Look, he's hot. I guess. The date won't be.

NATHAN. Sure it will. Two hotties, together? Hot date!

EVIE. He's going out with ME, not with –

NATHAN. That's what I said, chica caliente.

EVIE. Look, you don't have to be nice.

(He spins her around in the chair.)

(She looks at herself in the mirror, and her jaw drops.)

(She is, in fact, hot.)

Wow.

NATHAN. *(sing-song)* Somebody's gonna get lucky.

EVIE. Shut up!

(But she's smiling.)

TRANSITION: SE FUE NATHAN!

(SOLEDAD, another hairdresser, helps **NATHAN** *clean up, chattering.)*

SOLEDAD. Nunca voy a dejar que me ayudes a conocer hombres mas nunca, Nathan. En primer lugar, el idiota aparece tres horas tarde, y con cerveza barata. En ese momento pensé: "Olvídalo, no voy a salir con este idiota, pero he tenido una noche horrible, y pagué $75 pesos para un Brazillian y estoy bellaca con cojones. So, pensé, "Usalo, y mándalo para el (pal) carajo." Verdad? So... Estaba tragando tequila hasta que se puso suficientemente guapo para tirarmelo, y me dice que no se puede parar hasta que se lo marne! Y que hico? Término, meneando sobre mis jeans! Inmediatamente se puso los pantalones y se fue! Se fue Nathan! Y yo todavía estaba vestida!

NATHAN. ... What?

SOLEDAD. Stop pretending you're Latino!

NATHAN. I'm 1/8th Puerto Rican!

(They exit.)

ENORMOUS TASTE EXPLOSION IN MY MOUTH

(EVIE and RAUL enter EVIE (and KITTY's) apartment after their date. EVIE is soaking wet and shivering… and tipsy. RAUL has his coat over her.)

EVIE. I'm so sorry, you must have been so embarrassed –

RAUL. Me? I wasn't the one who made that spectacular splash…

EVIE. I was trying to be quirky!

RAUL. Quirky?

EVIE. And you know. Prance gracefully along the edge of the fountain, not fall in!

RAUL. Is that what you were doing.

EVIE. And my hair. Oh, my hair's all ruined. Nathan's masterwork, poof! In a splash! Gone! Oh, I was having such a good time, you know.

RAUL. Me too. Still am.

EVIE. You're so cute. Do people just give you stuff on the street when they see how cute you are?

RAUL. You really liked that plum wine, didn't you.

EVIE. Plum wine is amazing! Plums and wine together? Who would have thought that would create such an enormous taste explosion in my mouth?

(RAUL smiles at her.)

(beat)

I was nervous.

RAUL. Why?

EVIE. I've never done this before. Not really.

RAUL. Done what?

EVIE. Been on a date. Like, a real date. You know. Like, in real life.

RAUL. You're kidding.

EVIE. I'm not.

RAUL. No, I just mean like – I'm surprised. Why not? You're
great – you –

(fumbling)

You have such a big heart.

EVIE. It feels full right now. It actually… feels… I mean.
I write about it all the time. But it actually does.
I didn't realize. It actually feels…

*(She takes his hand and puts it on her chest. A moment.
She slowly brings it down again.)*

RAUL. Okay. Let's get you out of these clothes.

(She laughs, high-pitched and hysterical.)

You know what I mean. You should take a hot shower.

EVIE. Will you stay? I'll be right back.

RAUL. Of course.

*(**EVIE** gives him back his coat and goes into her room.
RAUL takes a look around and sits down on the couch.
He sits on something. He finds between the cushions – a
pair of handcuffs?)*

(We hear the shower turned on.)

*(The front door busts open and **RYAN** barges in.)*

Hey, woah.

RYAN. What. The Fuck!

*(**RAUL** quickly shoves the handcuffs back into the couch.)*

RAUL. Can I help you?

RYAN. Yeah, you can kiss my hairy ass, you sweet talking
assface.

RAUL. Who are you?

RYAN. I'm Evie's boyfriend, fuckertard.

RAUL. What?

RYAN. We're soulmates, you douchepervert.

RAUL. Wait a minute – what?

RYAN. Stay the fuck away from her.

RAUL. *(slowly)* That's up to her now, isn't it.

(**EVIE** *runs out in her towel.*)

EVIE. What's the – RYAN? What are you doing here?

RYAN. OH MY GOD.

EVIE. Ryan! Get out!

RYAN. You're naked!

EVIE. It's – not what it looks like. There was a fountain.

RYAN. You're gonna do him? When we're supposed to be 25 manning the Immortals together in the Graveyard Kingdoms? Bad enough you let me get decapitated the other day.

RAUL. ... What?

EVIE. Will you let that go already?

RYAN. That's what happens when you get distracted! And with this guy?

EVIE. Look, just –

RYAN. I heard you yesterday. I heard everything. I can't believe you'd do this to me.

EVIE. Ryan… I'm so sorry. I really didn't think you'd care. I…

RYAN. Of course I care! The guild's dropped down to the sixth worldwide because you've missed two nights of play in a row! What happened to your commitment?

EVIE. So it's just all about the game? That's it, isn't it. Nothing more?

RYAN. Well what the fuck do you want?

(pause)

EVIE. I don't wanna talk about this. I think you should leave.

RYAN. Really? With this guy? You thought this through?

EVIE. Just go.

RYAN. You really think he's gonna keep it in his pants just for you?

EVIE. SHUT UP.

(RAUL grabs RYAN's arm.)

RAUL. I think you should leave, man.

RYAN. Get off, assburger.

RAUL. Asperger? Like the syndrome?

RYAN. NO! ASS! BURGER! Like a burger made of ASS!

RAUL. Why didn't you just say that?

RYAN. I DID SAY THAT!

EVIE. Get out Ryan.

RYAN. You're out of the guild.

EVIE. Fine.

(RYAN is shocked.)

RYAN. I'M breaking up with YOU. You hear me? I dump YOU. Let the record show.

EVIE. Fine. Fantastic. Now leave. Please.

RYAN. *(to RAUL)*

You're wasting your time, man.

(RAUL practically shoves RYAN out the door, and closes it.)

EVIE. I'm sorry.

RAUL. Exciting evening.

EVIE. I really am.

RAUL. So you do have a boyfriend.

(EVIE hugs herself and sinks on to the couch, distraught.)

EVIE. I mean – we're not even really a couple. We don't even see each other, you know, like in real life, and he's – he's not very nice, and –

RAUL. Hey. It's… it's fine, I guess. I mean…

(Pause. She's upset. He sits next to her and puts a hand on her bare shoulder.)

Are you okay?

EVIE. Yeah.

(looking down at herself)

I guess you weren't expecting to see so much of me on a first date.

(She smiles up at him. She's adorable. He kisses her.)

RAUL. Is that okay?

EVIE. *(pause)* Yeah.

(Pause. She shifts, uncomfortable.)

What's –

(She pulls out the handcuffs from behind her and turns beet red.)

Kitty. What was she doing on this couch last night?

(RAUL quickly stands up.)

RAUL. Um, maybe we should –

(EVIE stands up.)

EVIE. Let's do this again?

(the smallest of beats)

RAUL. Yeah.

EVIE. Without the crazy person bursting in, or the wetness…

(He smiles, resisting.)

RAUL. Yeah. For sure.

(He's about to leave.)

EVIE. Hey.

(She kisses him on the cheek.)

You know what, actually –

(She kisses him on the lips.)

Yeah, okay.

RAUL. Okay.

(Pause. He kisses her again, properly.)

EVIE. Cool. My turn.

(She kisses him. She's not very good. She struggles to keep her towel up.)

RAUL. Do you want me to stay?

EVIE. Um.

RAUL. It's fine. Let's take it slow, yeah?

EVIE. Look – What he said. I mean – sometimes. Maybe. But – I could. I'm pretty good at picking up new skills. Hell, I went from level 1 to level 30 in a week and that's unheard of –

RAUL. Evie?

EVIE. Yes?

RAUL. I'll see you soon. Good night.

(He exits.)

(EVIE closes the door and leans against it. She feels her heart.)

(She feels her lips, and frowns.)

TRANSITION: DIVA CUP

(A sorority girl crosses the stage as she talks on her phone.)

TIPHANEÉ. Yeah, I wasn't expecting to do it last night. You know I'd been planning to do it for the first time on my birthday, you know, make it special. But my Diva Cup had just arrived! No, it's not for that, it's for your period. So I wanted to try it out to see if it would fit. But I couldn't like get it in, you know, I was like too tight. So Steven was there, and you know how he's been like wanting to do it ever since we started hanging out. So I was like Steven, do you wanna do it so I can stretch myself out. So like yeah we did it and it wasn't like super romantic or anything but now my Diva Cup fits!

(She exits.)

SHE GOT AN ASS LIKE UH UH UH.

(EVIE *sits at her usual spot outside the cafe, staring blankly at her latest client –* JERRY. *Young and enthusiastic.*)

JERRY. And she's got an ass like – mm! MM! MM!

EVIE. Okay. I get it. I think. But what do you want to <u>say</u> to her?

JERRY. And every time I see her I just wanna unh – unh – unh!

EVIE. This isn't helping!

JERRY. She likes to get freaky like wow, like unh, like – My girl is like – OWWWWWW!

EVIE. It hurts?

JERRY. So nasty. My girl she just hurtin' for a –

EVIE. Okay. I think I have enough.

JERRY. I told you about her ass right? I just wanna like

(mimes spanking an ass)

Uh-huh. Uh-huh. Uh-huh.

EVIE. Hold on, I didn't quite get that.

(typing)

Uh-huh. Uh-huh. Uh-huh.

JERRY. Her ass man, so, fffff – ggggnnhhh, mMM! Her ass is outta this WORLD!

EVIE. I just don't get it – you know, I try, I do – but I don't get this fascination with butts. I mean, Robert Burns never wrote about them. Shakespeare never did... I think. If Shakespeare never wrote about butts, then what right do I have?

(pause)

JERRY. So you gonna do this or what?

EVIE. It's a Facebook wall post. Just give me a second. And...

(She extends her hand and JERRY *pays her $10.)*

(KITTY enters just as JERRY gets up. They size each other up, very close, very horny.)

JERRY. Heeeeeey, baby.

KITTY. Yeah, I think so.

EVIE. Down, girl!

(KITTY reluctantly sits down. JERRY saunters away.)

Jimminy Cricket on a cracker. Is there no one on campus you've spared?

KITTY. It's been a month. I haven't found anyone else half as good. It's been… torture.

EVIE. The Geneva Convention didn't know the half of it.

KITTY. You wouldn't understand. God. Sometimes I think I'd be better off like you.

EVIE. I've been trying to tell you that for like four years now.

KITTY. This constant yearning is just driving me crazy!

(She writhes around on her chair.)

EVIE. Can't you like, you know, help yourself?

KITTY. It's not the same. Evie, I want him back.

EVIE. Really? Mommy issues and all?

KITTY. I don't care if he calls out for his mother. I don't care if he wants me to dress up like his mother. I just want him to fuck me like he used to.

(pause)

Please, Evie?

EVIE. Oh, come on Kitty. I barely have time for anything these days.

KITTY. You must have some time. Especially since you dumped that loser.

EVIE. I've kind of been seeing Raul.

KITTY. WHAT? That tall drink of hotness? What? And you didn't tell me?

EVIE. Well, you're never home, and it's kinda hard to have a conversation with you when you're doing… that.

(KITTY stops writhing and sits up straight.)

KITTY. *(breathy)* Okay. I'm all yours. Talk to me.

EVIE. Even the way you say that, you –

KITTY. Sorry. I can't turn it off sometimes. Okay. Tell me everything. What's he like? How good is he? What's his signature move?

EVIE. We haven't.

KITTY. But you've been seeing each other for what –

EVIE. A month, yeah.

KITTY. And you still haven't –

EVIE. We just haven't felt the need to.

KITTY. You mean YOU haven't. Jesus Evie, he's hot.

EVIE. I know. I'm very aware of how hot he is. He's so pretty I can't look at him directly sometimes.

(pause)

And it's not just that. He's wonderful. He takes care of me, you know? He cares.

KITTY. And he wants you.

EVIE. He's… indicated that.

KITTY. And so? Why not?

(pause)

Evie. He's not Ryan. Or anyone else. He's… this is your time. Finally.

EVIE. But, I don't… I don't want to.

KITTY. Why not?

EVIE. I don't like it.

KITTY. How do you know if you haven't even tried?

EVIE. We tried a little bit. I'm not really… feeling it. I like cuddling. Cuddling's awesome.

KITTY. Seriously?

EVIE. We just cuddle for hours sometimes.

KITTY. That's all you've done?

(pause)

You know a low libido can be a symptom of hypothyroidism. Or herpes.

EVIE. Well, my thyroid is fine.

(pause)

I just want to keep things as they are. Things are great right now. But I don't know how to... tell him that.

KITTY. You're being so stupid, you know that? Sex is amazing. All that stuff you write about for your clients, don't you want to experience it? That incredible anticipation where you can't sit still, where you can't think, you can't breathe. That moment when you let go and you lose control. That feeling you have when you're pleasuring someone and they're completely... yours.

EVIE. That's pretty good.

(writing)

I think I might use that –

KITTY. STOP DOING THAT.

EVIE. Doing what?

KITTY. Just writing about it! Do it!

EVIE. I don't want to, and I don't need to. Some people feel the need to go sky-diving, and I don't. I think my life will be just fine without it.

KITTY. Okay for the millionth time. How do you know that you won't like it, or love it, really, if you've never tried?

EVIE. Because I know. You wouldn't ask a gay guy if he's really sure that he's gay, just because he's never slept with a woman.

KITTY. Are you gay?

EVIE. No. I'm pretty much equal opportunity not interested.

KITTY. Are you sure you're not gay?

EVIE. Kitty...

KITTY. You sure you don't want some of this?

EVIE. Kitty –

KITTY. You swear you've never pictured it?

EVIE. Kitty! There are people here –

(KITTY kisses EVIE, expertly.)

KITTY. Well?

EVIE. *(pause)* Eh.

KITTY. Seriously?

EVIE. Well, now I know what your tongue tastes like.

KITTY. Nothing?

EVIE. It's not you, it's me. I think we've established that.

KITTY. Have I lost my gift? Is that what's going on?

EVIE. *(looking around the cafe)* Maybe now they'll make my lattes faster.

KITTY. I convert straight girls, you know that? Even if I'm not gay, they go gay for me!

EVIE. Are you okay?

KITTY. You don't get to tell me that it was 'eh'! You don't! I'm awesome! I'm really good at this!

EVIE. You're more than just your sexuality, you know.

KITTY. I'll see you later.

EVIE. Kitty – don't be angry –

KITTY. *(angry)* I'm not!

(She starts to storm out, then runs into JERRY again.)

You, me. Ladies room. Right now.

(He follows her with glee.)

EVIE. You have a girlfriend! With an ass like uh – uh – uh, remember?

(He shushes her as he follows KITTY out.)

DO YOU WANNA SEE MY PORTAL OF SECRETS

(In EVIE's room. EVIE lies back on her couch, legs out in front of her, laptop on her lap, typing rapidly.)

(RAUL sits on the floor, leaning against the couch by EVIE's legs, working on his homework. With a drafting notebook, an actual analog calculator, and pencils.)

(RAUL stretches, and reaches comfortably for EVIE's bare foot. He rubs it. EVIE giggles.)

EVIE. That tickles.

RAUL. Oh yeah?

(She giggles harder, then jerks her legs away.)

EVIE. Stop, you're distracting me.

(Typing. RAUL moves his hand to her leg, and massages it.)

RAUL. How's that?

EVIE. That's perfect.

(A moment. They look at each other.)

RAUL. What's up?

EVIE. *(smiling)* I like looking at you.

(She glances away from him, notices something on her computer. Starts typing again.)

RAUL. Still working on your Shakespeare paper?

EVIE. Hmm. No.

RAUL. Writing a letter for a client?

EVIE. Hmm.

RAUL. Why don't you read it out to me?

EVIE. What?

RAUL. Read it out. I love hearing your stuff. More interesting anyway than figuring out the stupid stress concentrations on a piston pump.

EVIE. Mm. Not writing a letter.

RAUL. Are you playing Warcraft again?

(*pause*)

Doesn't sound like you are.

EVIE. Uh. Playing in silent mode.

RAUL. I thought we were doing homework.

EVIE. We are! I'm just taking a break.

RAUL. Well, why didn't you tell me? I'm ready to take a break.

(*He kisses her foot.*)

(**EVIE** *laughs/shrieks and jerks away again.*)

EVIE. Ew! What are you doing?

RAUL. I'm sick of homework.

(*He pulls himself on to the couch and gets closer to* **EVIE**.)

EVIE. Raul – Kitty said she might come home tonight –

RAUL. She's not here yet. Come on. Let's take a break.

(**EVIE** *sits up, alert.*)

EVIE. Okay. Do you wanna get your laptop? We can play together.

RAUL. That's not really what I had in mind.

EVIE. Please? I set it up for you on your computer, why don't we just try?

RAUL. There are so many better things we could be doing with our time.

EVIE. Like what?

(*He kisses her.*)

Look, we'll do it PVP, okay, player – versus – player. That way you get to play with someone else. It's so much better with someone else, trust me.

RAUL. Oh, I believe you.

(*He kisses her again.*)

EVIE. Do you wanna see my portal of secrets?

RAUL. Hell yeah.

(She shifts away from him and shows him her laptop screen.)

EVIE. See that? That's where I am right now. I have to slay the Wizard highlord and his henchmen at the base of Mt. Carnage to get to the Portal of Secrets. And then it's mine!

(pause)

Dammit, Ryan's online. What's he doing?

(RAUL starts massaging her shoulders.)

RAUL. You don't wanna play with Ryan.

EVIE. No, I wanna play with you. *(pause)* That feels good.

RAUL. Yeah?

EVIE. Oh, my.

(pause)

That's, uh –

(looks at the screen)

Oh, no what's happening?

(She starts typing.)

(RAUL reaches around and shuts her laptop screen.)

Wait –

RAUL. Maybe you should stop playing. Like, seriously.

(pause)

You're in front of the computer all the time.

EVIE. But – I told you – It's been really hard for me ever since Ryan kicked me out of the guild. I've had to pay for my own repairs, figure out new strats for the raids, hook up with noobs who keep screwing up – I even had to trade my dragon for gold.

RAUL. But that's not real!

EVIE. It is to me.

RAUL. Well that's just weird!

EVIE. It's not that weird.

RAUL. You just told me you traded your dragon for gold! That's kinda weird!

EVIE. Well, when you say it like that, it just sounds stupid!

RAUL. How do you want me to say it? You're living in a fantasy.

EVIE. I'm not weird, okay. And I'm not stupid –

RAUL. When did I – I didn't say that.

EVIE. Why are we fighting?

RAUL. I don't know!

> *(beat)*

EVIE. Do you really want me to stop playing?

RAUL. I just – I just want to spend time with you.

EVIE. So do I.

RAUL. In real life.

> *(A pause. EVIE puts her laptop on the floor.)*

EVIE. We could do real life stuff. We could cosplay – you know – costume play? I could dress up as my avatar, Princess Azareth!

RAUL. You're not getting it.

EVIE. I have one for you too. It's another warrior princess one, you could show off your legs.

RAUL. No – what? No!

EVIE. Okay. What do you wanna do?

RAUL. What do you think?

> *(pause)*

Why won't you just let me–

> *(pause)*

Do you know what today is?

EVIE. What?

RAUL. It's been a month. Our first date –

EVIE. The 16th. You're right. It's like an anniversary.

RAUL. It is an anniversary.

> *(pause)*

Sometimes I feel like the girl in this relationship.

EVIE. It's a relationship?

RAUL. Yes, it is.

EVIE. I like you so much, you know?

(They kiss.)

(EVIE looks at him, eyes wide.)

(They kiss.)

RAUL. What do you want me to do?

EVIE. I – I don't know.

RAUL. Tell me what you want.

(He kisses her neck.)

EVIE. You know that back rub was nice.

RAUL. Mmhmm.

EVIE. Y – yeah.

(He starts unbuttoning her shirt and kissing down her chest. She squirms out from underneath him and tumbles on to the ground.)

No, no I can't.

(She starts buttoning up her shirt.)

RAUL. Hey – woah – hey I'm sorry. I didn't –

EVIE. It's not your fault, it's mine – it – it – it's not you it's me! Haha.

RAUL. What?

EVIE. It's – I should have told you. I should've.

RAUL. Told me what?

(pause)

Did... something happen to you?

EVIE. No! God no. Nothing like that.

RAUL. You can tell me.

EVIE. No, I just...

(pause)

(EVIE sits on the couch.)

RAUL. I like you too, Evie. You know that, right? A lot.

(**RAUL** *takes her hand. A moment.*)

EVIE. This is nice. I like this. I like your hand. It's big and it's interesting and it's warm and – this is nice. I feel… safe.

RAUL. I want you to feel safe.

(*pause*)

Are you gonna break up with me?

EVIE. No! No, I'm not. But you might.

RAUL. Why?

EVIE. Every time we kiss, and it starts… going somewhere… I – I can't – I can't do it.

RAUL. Want what exactly?

EVIE. Sex. Anything leading up to sex, even.

RAUL. I don't…

(*pause*)

Is it a religious thing?

EVIE. No.

RAUL. Seriously, did something happen to you?

EVIE. No. It's just. It's me. You know?

RAUL. So you've never…

EVIE. No.

RAUL. I know the first time can be scary. But it doesn't have to be scary with me.

EVIE. It's not about you. I'm just – I don't want to.

RAUL. Ever?

EVIE. …Yeah.

(*pause*)

RAUL. Is it a medical thing?

EVIE. No! Just hear me, okay.

RAUL. I'm hearing you. I just… don't get it. That letter you wrote for me. It was so… passionate. 'Your every touch fills me with a rush of joy so powerful –"

RAUL. I'm hearing you. I just... don't get it. That letter you
wrote for me. It was so... passionate. 'Your every touch
fills me with a rush of joy so powerful –"

EVIE. It's just words. I make up words, that's what I do. And
that wasn't me, it was for your ex.

(pause)

RAUL. So you're not attracted to me –

EVIE. I am! I – I am. You're so. I am. It's just – it's all here.
See? In my heart.

(She takes his hand and places it on her chest.)

My heart is full when I'm with you.

(RAUL looks at his hand on her chest longingly.)

RAUL. Evie...

EVIE. I know. And I don't blame you. I understand.
Completely.

RAUL. I'm not breaking up with you. Do you want me to?

EVIE. No!

RAUL. Then just –

(He pulls away and gets up, frustrated.)

Just. Let me think.

(pause)

So it's not me?

EVIE. It's not you. I'm just... I mean, some avatars can only
absorb and mitigate damage, you can't expect them to
pop a pyroblast with a mage stick as well.

RAUL. What?

EVIE. Everyone's different.

RAUL. But you're not... an avatar. That's not how this
works.

EVIE. It makes sense if you think about it.

(pause)

I wish you'd play. It's so much fun if you'd just give it
a try.

RAUL. I know something else that could be a lot of fun if you just…

(She doesn't care for the joke.)

(He goes back to her on the couch.)

EVIE. Look, I'm just trying to be honest here.

(pause, voice breaking)

I'm crazy about you but I can't… I can't keep you if you… If I can't…

RAUL. It's okay. It's okay.

(Pause. He looks at her laptop.)

So you want us to be together, but no sex?

EVIE. Can you do that?

RAUL. Can you stop playing that game?

EVIE. What? Raul, I – that's – that's not –

RAUL. I don't think it's that big a deal.

(pause)

Considering what you're asking.

(a long, terrifying moment)

EVIE. Okay.

(RAUL kisses her.)

RAUL. Wait, can I kiss you?

EVIE. *(happy)* Yeah.

(They kiss again. EVIE ends it, and snuggles into his arms.)

(pause)

This is great. This is going to be so great.

(beat)

(RAUL looks down at her. And shifts discreetly on the couch.)

RAUL. *(not convincingly)* Yeah.

End of Act I. Maybe.

MESSED UP

(Outside the cafe. EVIE *sits at her usual spot, maybe drinking tea, reading an actual book.)*

(Her eyes flicker around every few seconds. Her fingers and legs start twitching. She's going through withdrawal.)

(Her phone rings. She looks at it, confused. She answers.)

EVIE. Hello?

*(*RYAN *appears on the other end, headset on, at his laptop.)*

RYAN. What's up, loser.

EVIE. Why are you calling?

RYAN. You haven't been online in three days. You're not my girlfriend anymore, but I wanted to check and see if you were dead.

EVIE. I'm not dead. I'm just… taking a break.

RYAN. What?

EVIE. I'm busy.

RYAN. Bullshit. I'm looking up your stats right now. Do you have any idea where your DPS levels are at?

EVIE. Don't tell me.

RYAN. Jesus, I didn't think you'd go off the deep end when I kicked you out of the guild.

EVIE. *(very irritated)* It's not you.

RYAN. You know we ran Immortal Valiant the other day. The new portal unlocked for Chai. Could have been yours.

EVIE. You raided Immortal WITHOUT ME?

RYAN. Hey man you made your bed. Now you can just slash sleep in it.

EVIE. Whatever. I'm done. This whole game is a waste of time.

RYAN. *(shocked)* I'm gonna pretend you didn't just say that.

EVIE. Goodbye, Ryan.

RYAN. Wait!

> *(pause)*

> I... may consider taking you back into the guild.

EVIE. *(pause)* No thanks.

RYAN. What the fuck? What are you trying to pull here?

EVIE. Nothing! I have to stop playing, that's all.

RYAN. *(pause)* For what? For loverboy? Really? You know it's not gonna last. And in the meantime your gear is rusting, your DKP is depleting, and you're losing crucial alliances.

EVIE. For God's sake what if I want to try living in the real world for a change?

RYAN. What's the first rule of Warcraft?

EVIE. Never stand in the fire –

RYAN. – Never stand in the fire! And what are you doing? You're getting in over your head with some douchebucket titnozzle who doesn't even get you.

EVIE. He gets me –

RYAN. Then why does he want you to stop playing? Sounds like a dick.

EVIE. Because if I don't change, Ryan, I'm just gonna be goddamn stuck here forever. Because sometimes you have to stand in the fire to grow the fuck up.

RYAN. You're gonna come running back to me, just wait and see.

> **(EVIE** *hangs up.* **RYAN** *exits.)*

> **(EVIE** *tries to get back to her book. Can't. Notices someone.)*

EVIE. Kitty!

> **(KITTY** *saunters over, coffee in hand.)*

KITTY. Hey.

EVIE. Where have you been? Did you even come home this weekend? I tried calling.

KITTY. Massive bio test this morning. Massive hangover.

(**KITTY** *finally looks at her*)

What the fuck happened to you? You look like an English Lit major.

EVIE. I am an English Lit major.

(**EVIE** *pats the spot next to her.* **KITTY** *sits down.*)

EVIE. How was the test?

KITTY. Fine.

EVIE. *(pause)* So what happened with Mason? Did you send that email I wrote for you?

(pause)

Come on. No one can resist that. Or you.

KITTY. He replied.

(reading from her phone)

"Dear Kitty. I'm very flattered. This is very sweet of you. But I'm seeing someone else now. All the best, Mason."

(pause)

"All the best."

(pause)

I saw him at the test this morning. Sticking his tongue down some hoochie from Organic Chem.

EVIE. I'm sorry.

(pause)

It was just sex with him, you can get that from anyone.

KITTY. It's not the same. We understood each other. There weren't any expectations.

(pause)

What do I do now?

EVIE. Move on?

KITTY. Great advice. Thanks.

EVIE. Look, my relationship with Ryan was just like that – we understood each other – and you wanted me to break up with him.

KITTY. That's different. You're with an actual fucking guy now, that you can actually fucking make out with!

(pause)

And you're not even doing that, are you?

EVIE. Raul's... agreed to keep sex off the table, but I can't trust that he actually means it. I keep waiting him to explode or something...

KITTY. Oh my god. It's gonna happen. You think a guy's just gonna put up and shut up and turn into a monk just for you?

EVIE. Look, I'm –

KITTY. You have a good thing going. Don't screw this relationship up like you did mine.

EVIE. Kitty. That's not fair.

KITTY. Why did I listen to you? You don't even – you don't even want any of this. What the hell kind of advice can you give about real relationships if you can't even be in one?

(EVIE is shocked.)

Oh – don't. Don't look at me like that.

EVIE. It doesn't need sex to be a real relationship. Maybe you're the one who's messed up, Kitty. Maybe you're the one who doesn't know what she's talking about.

KITTY. *(angry)* Yeah. Whatever.

(KITTY gets up.)

EVIE. Kitty –

KITTY. Enjoy celibacy.

(KITTY leaves. EVIE is frustrated. She stuffs her book into her backpack. She feels a familiar object. Oh no.)

(She takes out her laptop.)

(She looks around. Worried, guilty. Opens the laptop, and starts to play.)

EVIE. *(sighing)* Fuck it.

SHHH

*(EVIE and RAUL are watching a movie, in a movie
theatre. Sitting in rows behind them and in front of them
respectively are a MAN and a WOMAN.)*

*(EVIE is a little on edge. She reaches for the popcorn and
accidentally touches RAUL. She jerks back.)*

RAUL. *(whispering)* I'm not trying to do anything.

EVIE. I'm just trying to get comfortable.

*(They both reach for the popcorn and their hands graze
again. EVIE jerks back again.)*

RAUL. *(exasperated)* Just take the popcorn.

EVIE. I don't want the whole thing.

RAUL. You've been acting weird all day.

EVIE. I have not.

(The MAN and the WOMAN "SHH" them.)

RAUL. Sorry.

*(They watch the movie. RAUL stretches and drapes his
arm over her chair. EVIE stiffens.)*

I can't put my arm around you now?

EVIE. Sure you can. It's a free country.

RAUL. Look – Evie – what happened this morning – it's
normal. It really is. Okay? Sometimes it happens.
Sometimes men wake up with an erection. It doesn't
mean anything.

EVIE. We fall asleep on the couch and I wake up feeling
this... thing... behind me.

RAUL. It was unintentional! A lot of erections are
unintentional, believe me.

EVIE. Were you... thinking about... me?

(The MAN and the WOMAN "SHHH" them.)

RAUL. Sorry.

(pause, whispering)

Of course. I think about you all the time.

EVIE. I can't, Raul. You know I can't.

RAUL. I know.

EVIE. Then why do you do it?

RAUL. I can't help how I feel.

EVIE. Well – then – just… Just do it with someone else.

RAUL. What?

EVIE. Look. It's not fair to expect you to turn into a monk just because I want you to. Just because I don't want sex doesn't mean you can't have any.

RAUL. Evie, stop talking like that. I don't want to –

EVIE. Look, I'm giving you permission. I just don't need to hear the details. But whatever makes you happy.

RAUL. This isn't what I want –

EVIE. Well then what do you want me to do?

MAN. Will you shut up? We're trying to watch a movie here!

EVIE. Yes, I'm sure you came to see Transformers 5 for the dialogue.

WOMAN. Stop talking about your sex lives in the theatre! What is wrong with you kids? Don't you have Facebook for that?

MAN. I know, right? We're trying to watch some wholesome family fare here.

EVIE. And Megan Fox just took her top off.

(Everyone immediately swivels around to look at the screen.)

(beat)

RAUL. Anyway we don't have a sex life.

(EVIE looks at him.)

(RAUL shifts in his seat.)

(They continue watching the movie.)

IT'S NOT DISEASED, IT'S JUST DEFECTIVE

(EVIE *sits in an OB/GYN's office, with the* DOCTOR, *who's older, maternal.* EVIE *sits on the examining table, and has a paper sheet draped across her lap.*)

EVIE. I think something's wrong with my vagina.

DOCTOR. Why do you say that?

EVIE. I think it's defective. What's the warranty on this thing? I demand a refund.

DOCTOR. *(checking her chart)* Is this your first pelvic exam?

EVIE. Yep.

DOCTOR. You seem tense.

EVIE. I'm confused.

DOCTOR. Why do you say your vagina is defective?

EVIE. I just... can't... stand... anyone... touching it.

DOCTOR. Okay.

EVIE. Or... doing... anything... near it...

DOCTOR. All right.

EVIE. Or... thinking about it.

DOCTOR. I see.

EVIE. You're thinking about it right now.

DOCTOR. It's my job.

EVIE. Of course.

DOCTOR. Have you been checked out for a UTI?

EVIE. It's not diseased, it's just defective.

DOCTOR. Do you masturbate?

EVIE. *(horrified)* Why would I DO that to myself? It's bad enough he...

DOCTOR. He?

EVIE. My boyfriend.

   (pause)

   Something's wrong down there.

DOCTOR. Would you like me to check?

EVIE. Yes. If you'd like.

DOCTOR. Lie back.

(EVIE *lies back.*)

DOCTOR. Try to relax.

EVIE. Trying.

DOCTOR. As you can see, I'm wearing gloves. I'm applying lubrication. Remember to continue breathing.

(EVIE *breathes loudly and excessively.*)

Well, everything looks fine.

EVIE. Okay. AHHHHH.

DOCTOR. Just relax. That was your clitoris. No swelling or abnormalities. You're fine.

EVIE. Why does it – why do I hate it then?

DOCTOR. Do you feel discomfort when you wear underwear? When you walk? Cross your legs?

EVIE. No.

DOCTOR. Then it's all your head.

EVIE. It can't be. It can't.

DOCTOR. Remember to keep breathing. I am now inserting my index finger into your vaginal canal.

(EVIE *yelps.*)

Yes, your hymen is intact, you may experience some tearing and discomfort –

(EVIE *yelps.*)

– the first time you –

(EVIE *yelps.*)

You attempt to –

(EVIE *yelps.*)

DOCTOR. Remember, lubricant is your friend.

(EVIE *yelps, and yelps, and squeals.*)

(*She stops. Is still.*)

*(The **DOCTOR** is removing her gloves. The test is over.)*

EVIE. What was that?

DOCTOR. Nothing to worry about, hon. You just had an orgasm.

EVIE. What?

DOCTOR. You had an orgasm.

EVIE. But – no. No. No.

DOCTOR. Evie, calm down.

EVIE. No. No, no, no, no.

*(**EVIE** pulls on her skirt, grabs her bag, and runs out of the **DOCTOR**'s office.)*

A BAD IDEA

(A bar.)

*(**KITTY** enters from the bathroom, hair and clothes in disarray. She heads straight to the bar, and taps her empty shot glass on the counter.)*

KITTY. Another.

(As she waits, she sees an abandoned drink nearby. She downs it.)

*(**RAUL** walks by, in a similar state of inebriation.)*

RAUL. Kitty.

KITTY. Hey. You!

RAUL. Hey.

*(**KITTY** starts laughing. She gets up, stumbles a bit, and hugs him.)*

KITTY. How are you?

*(**RAUL** helps her back to her bar stool and sits next to her.)*

RAUL. Just great.

KITTY. So nice to see a friendly face.

RAUL. You here with Evie?

KITTY. No. Evie skeevy.

RAUL. What?

KITTY. Nothing. You're not here with Evie?

RAUL. No.

KITTY. She should be careful. A lotta drunk girls here tonight.

RAUL. That's not an issue, apparently.

KITTY. What?

RAUL. She doesn't care. Says… I can do what I want.

KITTY. Anything you want? Anyone you want?

RAUL. Pretty much.

KITTY. Evie… is such an idiot sometimes.

RAUL. Why do you say that?

KITTY. I tell her not to screw this up, and she tells you to screw other girls? The fuck is she thinking?

RAUL. I don't know.

(*pause*)

What's wrong?

KITTY. We had a fight. And it was really my fault. But she's frustrating. A frustrator. Frustrates –

RAUL. What?

KITTY. I'm losing my touch, Raul. And I'm not getting satisfied.

RAUL. How drunk are you?

KITTY. I'm just a little…

(*pause*)

RAUL. I just want her. All of her. And if she doesn't want to be with me – that way – then maybe she just doesn't want to be with me.

(*pause*)

I keep trying, you know – I just always – man. I always keep trying. And they're never happy.

KITTY. Fuck you. You're terrific.

(*pause*)

And so is she.

RAUL. She really is.

KITTY. I love her to bits.

RAUL. Me too. This isn't fair.

KITTY. She doesn't get it. She should just get off that damn computer already and ride you like a carousel horse –

RAUL. Wait –

KITTY. Sorry, was that crude?

RAUL. She's still playing the game?

(*stunned*)

Fuck.

KITTY. Oh my God!

(**KITTY** *practically slides off her bar stool.* **RAUL** *catches her.*)

RAUL. Are you okay?

KITTY. Freshman orientation!

RAUL. What?

KITTY. That's where we met. The ice – breaker.

(*a moment*)

RAUL. Do you have someone to take you home?

(*They stare at each other.*)

(*Lights dim.*)

THEY SAY THE WAITING MAKES IT BETTER

(EVIE *sits with* CHARLOTTE, *a new client, primly dressed.*)

EVIE. All right. How about... When I look at you... I see... the person... who... completes me.

(CHARLOTTE *is skeptical.*)

Sorry. Sorry. Joking. Obviously. Umm. Okay. How about... On this day, our special day, when I look into your eyes... I realize... you... complete me.

CHARLOTTE. Can we get off Jerry Maguire just for a little bit?

EVIE. I'm sorry. I really – I just. I'm having a bad morning.

CHARLOTTE. That's okay, but... my wedding's tomorrow.

EVIE. I'll get this done, I swear.

CHARLOTTE. Look, I don't need anything fancy. I'm just not a writer. He's the one who wanted us to write our own vows. I would have been happy with the traditional stuff, love, honor and obey. You know. Keep it simple.

EVIE. Obey? Really?

(*Again, that look.*)

EVIE. Sorry. Not my place.

CHARLOTTE. Look, I... I love him. I cannot wait to be married to him. I mean – I really – I cannot wait for tomorrow. I've been waiting for three years now.

EVIE. Wow, you've been engaged for three years?

CHARLOTTE. No, I've been dating him for three years. I've been waiting, well, actually... for a lot longer than that.

EVIE. Oh. OH. Oh, I see.

CHARLOTTE. Yeah.

EVIE. Wow. Big night tomorrow, huh.

CHARLOTTE. You could say that.

EVIE. You, uh... you looking forward to it?

CHARLOTTE. Well, yeah, of course. Who wouldn't?

EVIE. It's just that... well, uh... you did choose not to –

CHARLOTTE. Well that's what God wants. But between you and me, I have been playing the scene over and over in my head. Imagining him… and me finally… you know. I'm not sure if that's a sin. But… God… it just… my married friends, they're like… they say it's worth it, you know, they say the waiting actually makes it better.

EVIE. Uh huh.

CHARLOTTE. But let me tell you, I've been tempted. Boy have I been tempted. You're not Christian, are you?

EVIE. No.

CHARLOTTE. I'm nervous too. What if I do something wrong? What if it sucks?

EVIE. You'll be fine. You're getting married. It has to work, right?

CHARLOTTE. "We'll be fine. We're getting married. It has to work, right?" That's not a bad start.

EVIE. I'm sorry.

CHARLOTTE. I don't mean to be a you-know-what, but I did ask you like two weeks ago.

EVIE. I've been having a really weird extended case of writer's block. I just… for weeks now I haven't been able to… find the words. The words are gone.

CHARLOTTE. What happened?

EVIE. I don't know… well, maybe I do. I've been seeing this guy… and the more intense it gets… the less I'm able to write. It's strange.

CHARLOTTE. Maybe it's all the sex. Have you ever considered waiting?

(EVIE *goes quiet. Distant.*)

Hello?

EVIE. Charlotte… were you ever scared?

CHARLOTTE. Of what?

EVIE. Of – of sex. Of the fact that – that you have to do it one day. That you thought you knew yourself, and you had a reason for not – not having to do it – but the more time goes on you realize – that – that reason doesn't exist anymore, and now you have to make a choice, you don't have an excuse.

CHARLOTTE. Uh, that's… not how we think of it, if that's what you're asking

EVIE. No, I don't mean you as a Christian, I mean you as a person. Are you scared about tomorrow?

CHARLOTTE. I'm nervous, but not… scared? No. God wants me to experience this. It's why… that's why it exists. That's why we exist.

EVIE. For sex? Nothing else?

CHARLOTTE. Well, I mean, it's one of the reasons. It's a big reason.

EVIE. *(pause)* I guess, I kind… of… I wish I had your faith. Not necessarily in God even, just… in tomorrow. In what you're going to do tomorrow. The faith that it's going to be okay. And you're not going to be hurt. And that it's the right thing.

CHARLOTTE. It's the right thing when it's with the right person. That's what I believe. And that's why I think God wants us to wait.

EVIE. Okay. Yeah. I guess I get that.

CHARLOTTE. You just have to… remember that… sex is the most intimate act humans are capable of – it's special. You need to be with someone who's patient, and kind… Who believes in you. Encourages you. Wants you to… be the best version of yourself. Because that's what he sees… that's who he sees when he looks at you. And all you want to do is be that person. Because you feel the same way about him.

(pause)

You know what I'm saying?

EVIE. You're right.

(pause)

And I think… I know what you're going to say tomorrow.

(She smiles at CHARLOTTE *and starts writing.)*

COSPLAY

(*RAUL's apartment. The doorbell rings. And rings. RAUL comes out of his bedroom, putting his shirt on.*)

(*He opens the door. EVIE enters, covered up in a trenchcoat, wearing a crazy wig.*)

RAUL. Hey. Hey – Evie – uh

EVIE. Wait – I know I look weird, but – check it out –

(*She takes off her coat.*)

(*She's dressed in her Pricess Azareth costume. In straddling the fine line between sexy and dorky, she falls ever so slightly on the sexy side.*)

Ta da!

(*beat*)

RAUL. What is that?

EVIE. It's my avatar! I'm Princess Azareth. Look – I know you don't like this stuff – but check it out. Don't I look good?

RAUL. Wow.

EVIE. I look good, right?

RAUL. You look… amazing. Crap.

EVIE. I kind of ran out of material when I was making it –

RAUL. L – looks fine to me.

EVIE. I've been thinking, Raul, that you've been very patient with me. I'm ready to give this a real shot. For you.

RAUL. What?

EVIE. Let's make love.

(*She pushes him on to the couch and gets on top of him.*)

RAUL. Woah, Evie.

EVIE. Let's do it!

(*She kisses him with a whole lot of show. She stops. She gets up and looks at him.*)

You just had sex.

RAUL. What? That's. That –

EVIE. You just had sex.

RAUL. … How could… what makes you say that?

EVIE. You smell just like Kitty smells after she –

(*She realizes.*)

Oh my god. You smell like Kitty.

(*She opens the bedroom door.* KITTY *steps out, wrapped in a bedsheet.*)

KITTY. Hi.

(EVIE *turns around abruptly and makes for the door.* RAUL *stops her.*)

RAUL. Wait, don't go.

EVIE. The two of you – I can't even – how do you even – did you – have you been seeing each other?

RAUL. No –

KITTY. No –

RAUL. Not at all –

KITTY. Nothing like that – we were just at –

RAUL. We just happened to –

KITTY. To run into each other –

RAUL. At Terry's –

KITTY. That bar –

RAUL. You know the one –

KITTY. We were really, really drunk. Really, really – really –

EVIE. I got it. That's all it takes, doesn't it?

RAUL. No, I mean – yes – I mean –

KITTY. We were just talking. We weren't going to – or planning to –

RAUL. Really drunk.

KITTY. And I was thinking, again – where have I –

RAUL. Where we would have seen each other –

KITTY. Where have I seen him before –

RAUL. And we were just talking –

KITTY. And we figured –

RAUL. We figured it out –

KITTY. It was freshman –

RAUL. Freshman orientation.

KITTY. The ice-breaking session. We were in the same group.

EVIE. So?

KITTY. Look it means nothing, okay? You know me. Sex… it's like working out. You know? Or going on a ride at an amusement park. You don't get emotionally attached to a ferris wheel.

(*EVIE looks at* **RAUL.**)

It didn't mean anything to him too. I'm sure he was thinking of you the whole time. Were you?

RAUL. I feel like this is a trick question.

EVIE. I'm going.

RAUL. No, wait.

EVIE. What could you possibly have to say? Either of you?

(*beat*)

I thought so.

(*She turns to leave.*)

RAUL. Why are you mad?

EVIE. Are you… Did you just say that? Did you actually just say that?

RAUL. Why – why are you upset?

EVIE. You cheated on me and you're asking why I'm upset?

RAUL. I didn't cheat on you. You said this would be okay –

EVIE. NOT WITH HER!

RAUL. Well, you never said that –

EVIE. ARE YOU SERIOUS?

RAUL. We don't have sex in our relationship. I respect that. I totally – I try my best – You said this would be okay.

KITTY. Evie, he does have a point.

EVIE. You stay out of this!

KITTY. No! Why? No! I'm your best friend! I've been putting up with your weird sexual hang-ups for four years now!

EVIE. Like I haven't? For you? Look who's talking!

KITTY. Fine, so we're both a little extreme.

EVIE. Will you please put some clothes on!

(KITTY goes into the bedroom.)

(EVIE and RAUL look at each other, look away.)

(a long beat)

Was she good?

RAUL. What?

EVIE. Kitty. She must be good, right. She must be phenomenal. I mean, she certainly practices a lot.

RAUL. Don't be like that.

EVIE. So she was good. Of course she was. Of course.

(KITTY comes out, fully dressed.)

KITTY. Evie… I don't know what to say.

EVIE. That's fine. You don't have to say anything to me ever, really.

KITTY. That's harsh! Dude!

EVIE. We are through.

RAUL. I made the first move.

(They whirl on him.)

KITTY.   EVIE.
What?   What?

RAUL. I initiated it. Not Kitty. Not her – you shouldn't – you shouldn't blame her –

KITTY. Oh, come on.

EVIE. How noble of you. To throw yourself on your own sword for this slut.

(silence)

(**KITTY** *exits.*)

(*beat*)

RAUL. That was out of line.

(**EVIE** *stares. Then starts smacking him.*)

EVIE. Out of line? OUT OF LINE?

RAUL. Yes – you shouldn't have called her that –

EVIE. You're taking her side now?! You're taking her fucking side –

RAUL. It's not about sides! You just called your best friend a slut –

EVIE. I don't think you get to be on the high horse here –

RAUL. I didn't do anything wrong.

EVIE. What?

RAUL. How could I know you'd suddenly be ready?! That you'd suddenly want this after weeks of – two days ago you wouldn't let me touch you!

EVIE. That doesn't mean you go and sleep with my roommate!

RAUL. Fine – you're right – maybe it shouldn't have been her.

EVIE. It shouldn't have been anyone.

RAUL. Then why? Why did you say that? You know what? You set the fucking rules and I followed them! Unlike you.

EVIE. What?

RAUL. You're still playing that stupid game. You think I don't know?

(*a moment*)

EVIE. I can't believe you're comparing playing Warcraft to sleeping with Kitty –

RAUL. It's kinda the same thing, isn't it?

EVIE. That's insane. It's nothing like –

RAUL. You cheated. I didn't. You said this would be fine –

EVIE. It doesn't matter what I said you should have known better!

RAUL. Now I'm supposed read your mind too? Like I haven't done enough – like I haven't – any other guy – the moment you said no sex, he would have been out of there –

EVIE. Well then why didn't you go? Why did you stay? Why are this doing this to me?

(beat)

RAUL. There is something seriously wrong with you.

EVIE. I know.

RAUL. It's not what you think. You're… you're crazy. You're crazy. And you show up here, dressed like a freak and try to jump me and expect everything to be okay?

(silence)

(**EVIE** *looks down at her costume.*)

Evie…

(**EVIE** *exits.*)

ALL'S FAIR IN LOVE AND WARCRAFT UNIVERSE

(Inside Warcraft Universe. It's dark.)

(All movement and fighting inside Warcraft Universe must be stylized to resemble the game's actual moves. Trust me, it's hilarious.)

(We hear conversations going on from random gamers.)

RANDOM GAMER. Anyone got some healing potion for sale? I got 60 gold.

RANDOM GAMER. The next expansion's gonna suck!

RANDOM GAMER. Holy dongthwistle! Is that Princess Azareth?

RANDOM GAMER. Shit she's back in the realm?

RANDOM GAMER. I thought I saw a Night Elf with the Sabre of Truth like a week ago but I was sure I was like hallucinating.

RANDOM GAMER. Yo, Azareth, we heard you're guild shopping? We got a sweet spot open for you. No application necessary.

RANDOM GAMER. Wait a minute I thought she was banned on this server for pwning too hard.

RANDOM GAMER. Yeah, I heard she went to the starter area and killed… like… everyone. So many noobs died they had to reset the server.

RANDOM GAMER. LOL IKR. So many noobs cried the server collapsed under the weight of their tears.

*(Lights rise on **EVIE** as Princess Azareth. Magnificent, beautiful and bad-ass. We are inside a dungeon.)*

*(**RYAN** comes barreling in. He is a gnome avatar, and dressed as such.)*

RYAN. All clear, but the boss is on the approach. Remember to switch over to the necklace of Infinite Void for minus 30% shadow damage reduction.

EVIE. I know, I didn't spawn this avatar yesterday. Where's the rest of the team? I thought you recruited a couple of noobs?

RYAN. What the hell, where is everyone else? The DPS porting in or what? Shit! Great! What's the point of anything now?!

EVIE. Great to have you back too, Ryan.

(The monster attacks. They quickly fend it off but not before EVIE *makes a mistake and they take some damage.)*

RYAN. Nice going.

EVIE. Shut up.

RYAN. I don't see any point in letting you back into my guild if you're just gonna...

EVIE. Whatever. I'm focused. I'm here. I'm back. Let's kill some monsters.

(They stand on guard.)

RYAN. So what changed?

EVIE. What?

RYAN. Why did you beg me to let you back in?

EVIE. I did not beg you.

RYAN. Trouble in paradise with lover boy? Is that why you begged me –

EVIE. I did not –

RYAN. Is that why you're back?

EVIE. We broke up.

RYAN. Oh really. I told you so.

EVIE. Shut up. And don't get any ideas. This doesn't mean we're back together.

RYAN. Hey man, you don't get to decide. I'm the leader of the guild and I call the shots.

(The monster appears again. EVIE *and* RYAN *go on attack.)*

RYAN. Where the fuck are our damage dealers? We're two men down and we haven't even nuked the first boss!

(EVIE *and* RYAN *quickly deflect the monster. It hides.*)

Good. Nice. Nice.

EVIE. Did you miss me?

RYAN. Let me put it this way. Without your healer stats, the guild DPS dropped and it took us a whole 35 seconds to down the Fire Eagles.

EVIE. Thirty five seconds? Noob.

RYAN. Yeah. So. Glad to have you back.

EVIE. I'm touched.

(*Maybe she is.*)

RYAN. So real life didn't turn out so great, huh?

EVIE. Real life sucks.

RYAN. I hear ya.

EVIE. *(pause)* What do you want, Ryan? What do you really want?

RYAN. That's a good question.

(*pause*)

If I could just get my alchemy to max, I could totally create my vial of sands, and turn into a dragon so my friends could ride me.

(EVIE *sighs.*)

(*The monster rises again.*)

What? We can't keep getting hit, we're stacking too many debuffs –

(*Two other WU characters –* a SHAMAN *and a* PALADIN *– both female – run in just in time and together they take down the monster.*)

FINALLY! What took you guys so long?

SHAMAN. Chill out dude, I had to go repair and pick up water.

RYAN. What the hell, you could have just asked for mage food.

SHAMAN. Oh don't start on me little man, who died and made you Raid Leader?

RYAN. Get your i-Level above 350 and we'll talk.

EVIE. Guys, just quit it, we're fine.

PALADIN. Are you...

EVIE. Am I what? Why are you looking at me like that?

SHAMAN. Oh my God. You're her. You're – you're Princess Azareth.

EVIE. Uh. Yes? That's me.

SHAMAN. Wow. We've been looking for you for forever!

EVIE. Looking?

PALADIN. Uh – what she means is...

SHAMAN. We're big fans.

EVIE. Yeah?

SHAMAN. We've been looking for you for two weeks. This place is HUGE.

EVIE. But why were you looking for me?

(The monster is back.)

PALADIN. Stand back! I got this!

*(The **PALADIN** starts doing a silly dance.)*

What? Attack, dammit, attack!

SHAMAN. What are you doing?

PALADIN. *(still dancing)*

I'm trying to attack!

RYAN. WTF noob, L2P!

PALADIN. What?

RYAN. What the fuck, newbie, LEARN TO PLAY!

PALADIN. Why didn't you just say that?

RYAN. I DID SAY THAT!

(Dance dance –)

Stop that. Leave it to them. Just help me scour the perimeter.

(RYAN *leads the* PALADIN *out, they exit.*)

(EVIE *and the* SHAMAN *take down the monster.*)

EVIE. *(panting)* We make a good team.

SHAMAN. Of course we do. We always have. God, I miss you so much.

EVIE. Do I know you?

SHAMAN. It's me. Kitty.

EVIE. What. But how –

KITTY. This world is not easy to figure out, let me tell you –

EVIE. You – you – what are you doing –

KITTY. You don't come out of your room, you ignore me in class, you pretend like you don't know even fucking know me –

EVIE. And so you – you – infiltrate the one place I can get away from you?

KITTY. You've been wanting me to try this out for years –

EVIE. It doesn't matter because we're not friends anymore.

KITTY. Stop saying that!

EVIE. How dare you come in here – this is MY world, not yours, you can't screw me over here as well –

KITTY. I just want to talk to you –

EVIE. I challenge you to a duel.

KITTY. What?

EVIE. You heard me.

(*strikes a pose*)

Slash duel.

(KITTY *gasps. Automatically gets into the same pose.*)

KITTY. You sure you wanna do this?

EVIE. Bring it on.

(*They start fighting.* KITTY *is surprisingly good.* EVIE *struggles a bit.*)

KITTY. We could just settle this like civilized people –

EVIE. Not in my world.

KITTY. You won't even let me apologize –

EVIE. Stab me in the back why don't you –

KITTY. I didn't mean to betray you –

EVIE. No you actually stabbed me in the back! Dammit!

(EVIE*'s health points are depleting.*)

KITTY. Shit! Sorry! Does it hurt?

EVIE. This isn't real!

(*The duel has paused.*)

(*beat*)

How did you get so good?

KITTY. Dude, I told you. I've been playing this game for two weeks just trying to find you.

(*beat*)

EVIE. Wow.

KITTY. I miss you. I just want you to talk to me.

EVIE. I miss you too.

(*pause*)

I shouldn't have called you that – I shouldn't have…

KITTY. Can we ever be okay again?

EVIE. Why did you do it Kitty?

KITTY. I don't know. I really don't.

(*pause*)

I screwed up. But I need you. I love you, I – I'm sorry.

(*pause*)

EVIE. Slash hug.

KITTY. Slash hug.

(*They hug.*)

EVIE. So – dude – are you home right now?

KITTY. Yeah, I'm in my room.

EVIE. Oh, I didn't hear you.

KITTY. Wanna go get some fro – yo?

(RYAN and the PALADIN suddenly burst back into the scene, being chased by the monster.)

RYAN. Don't stand in the fire! Don't stand in the fire!

PALADIN. EVIE! Watch out!

(The PALADIN pushes her right into the line of fire. EVIE takes a hit.)

RYAN. What the hell?!

(The PALADIN is flailing.)

PALADIN. Shit! These stupid controls – Kitty!

RYAN. What?

KITTY. Fuck's sake Raul. It's Control T, not Control Y.

EVIE. Raul?

RYAN. What?!

(The PALADIN – RAUL – stops flailing. EVIE is still under attack)

RAUL. Evie – you okay?

EVIE. Shit – my health points – dammit.

(She reels and faints and "dies".)

RAUL. What just happened?

RYAN. She just died, crackerfart. Dammit, this sets us back like 16 points.

PALADIN. SHE DIED?

KITTY. She's not dead dead. She's been teleported to the graveyard, she needs to get back here on foot to continue the game.

(They hear the monster.)

RYAN. Goddammit and the boss is still breathing!

RAUL. Where's the graveyard?

KITTY. Where we came from, but –

(RAUL runs out of the dungeon.)

RYAN. Where the fuck are you going? Fuck!

(The monster roars from the darkness at the edges.)

RYAN. This is a wipe! Fucking! Okay – retreat –

KITTY. We're not gonna retreat, what are you a baby?

RYAN. But –

KITTY. Recon strat gamma lightblade.

RYAN. That's crazy no one does that anymore.

KITTY. You take a hit – and I bring it down from the back.

RYAN. We can't do that – our tank just died – we can't take any more hits –

KITTY. Stop being such a goddamn pussy!

(She shoves him out. She raises her sword and lets out a battle cry. She runs off in the direction of the monster.)

(TRANSITION TO… *The Graveyard.*)

(EVIE wakes up.)

EVIE. Ugh.

(RAUL runs in. Wearing the **PALADIN** *costume. Showing off his legs.)*

RAUL. Oh good, you're here.

EVIE. Raul? Is that really you?

(RAUL shrugs.)

RAUL. Are you okay?

EVIE. Yeah. I'm home. I'm fine.

RAUL. I mean – like – here –

EVIE. Well, I'm dead. I have to walk back to the dungeon or I don't get my health points back.

RAUL. Can I walk with you?

EVIE. What are you doing here?

RAUL. Kitty and I kinda got the same idea.

(EVIE winces.)

I'm so sorry for what I said. I feel terrible.

EVIE. Okay.

RAUL. That's it?

EVIE. Look, I just don't see what more we have to say to each other.

RAUL. But –

EVIE. I'm not saying it was your fault. You're right, I – I can't really blame you, you know –

RAUL. Why don't we both just say we screwed up, and try again?

(beat)

EVIE. I thought you hated this game.

RAUL. It's not that bad. I can – I can kinda see the appeal.

(He looks down at his clothes.)

EVIE. You chose to be an enchantress?

RAUL. A Paladin.

EVIE. Well, in the enchantress profession. Your skirt's kinda short.

(beat)

RAUL. So this is where you live, huh?

EVIE. Not in the graveyard.

RAUL. This world. I mean… I get it. I do. It's pretty fantastic.

EVIE. Maybe.

RAUL. You look so beautiful in this world. Powerful. Sexy. Just… like there's nothing you can't do.

EVIE. You see why I like it?

RAUL. But you're the same in the real world. I can see you sitting in your room, and you're beautiful and you're powerful and you're sexy. And I – I love you.

(beat)

EVIE. You look really good in that outfit.

RAUL. *(pause)* I like it.

EVIE. What?

RAUL. This… these clothes. I feel good. In them.

EVIE. You like dressing up? As a woman?

RAUL. *(whispering)* Yes.

EVIE. Why didn't you tell me before?

RAUL. Come on. I can't believe I'm telling you now.

(pause)

You're not the only with... issues, you know.

EVIE. It's cool. It's cute. It's cosplay. I love cosplay.

RAUL. You messing with me?

EVIE. No. You look good.

RAUL. *(pause)* I do, don't I.

EVIE. Yeah, but sorry. Time for it to go.

> (EVIE *pushes* RAUL *to the ground. She straddles his lap and kisses him.*)

RAUL. What are you doing?

EVIE. Slash kissing you. Slash undressing you. Slash –

RAUL. I get the picture.

EVIE. I love you.

RAUL. *(smiling)* Finally.

> (*He kisses her back.*)

> (*TRANSITION back to the dungeon.*)

> (RYAN *and* KITTY *emerge, bloodied and victorious.*)

KITTY. Well, that's that.

RYAN. I can't believe we just nuked a boss with two men down.

KITTY. Recon strat gamma lightblade. It works.

RYAN. How did you even know about that?

KITTY. A wizard taught me when I was a level 32. He was pretty hot. But turns out he's a priest in Finland.

> (*notices* RYAN *staring at her*)

What?

RYAN. Nothing, I just – nothing.

> (*They sit down, exhausted.*)

KITTY. Find your enemy's weakness and use it against them. Rule number two of –

RYAN. Warcraft. Yeah.

> (RYAN *splits a piece of bread and offers it to her.*)

Want some mage food?

KITTY. Gee. Thanks.

*(They eat the bread and look at each other. **KITTY** smiles.)*

TRANSITION: SIZE MATTERS

(Two Physics majors walk to class, talking shop.)

LUCAS. I just feel like particle physics isn't ready for the Large Hadron Collider. No point in rushing the whole process.

PEARL. It's not about being ready, it's all about size. Size is so important in penetrating undiscovered areas of Physics.

LUCAS. Size is overrated.

PEARL. Also they could avoid all their performance issues if they just turn on the beams slow at first, I mean it takes some time to warm up and then go faster and faster and faster until the stream of particles are released and scatter everywhere…

(They are the cutest. They exit.)

AND THEY LIVED...

(EVIE works at her usual spot outside the cafe.)

(RAUL enters. EVIE looks up. She's surprised, and hopeful. She smiles. RAUL smiles back. Relieved.)

RAUL. Hey.

EVIE. Hi.

RAUL. Can I...

EVIE. Sure.

(He sits down next to her.)

PAUL. How are you?

EVIE. Good. You?

RAUL. I was hoping I'd find you here.

EVIE. Well, I'm here.

(pause)

RAUL. What are you working on?

EVIE. Oh, just another letter.

RAUL. Okay.

EVIE. I'm having some trouble with this one.

(pause)

I used to think that words could solve anything. All you needed were the right commands, the right strategy... but then... what if people are too complicated for that? And what if... some problems just aren't meant to be solved?

RAUL. Well, what have you got so far?

EVIE. Well. Okay.

(She reads:)

My dear...

(She stops, smiles, embarrassed.)

RAUL. Go on.

EVIE. My dear Raul.

(RAUL *smiles.*)

I admit that I'm scared. I admit that for my whole life, I've lived in my mind and feared my body. I admit that I'm terrified of getting hurt. I admit that the way you look at me is overwhelming and overpowering and I don't like not being in control. I know that life will be a lot easier if I don't stand in the fire, but maybe... it's time that I took a chance and just got burnt.

(beat)

First draft.

RAUL. Will you have dinner with me, Evie?

EVIE. Tonight?

RAUL. Yeah.

EVIE. Like, a date?

RAUL. Yeah.

EVIE. Are you sure?

RAUL. I'll kiss you good night at the door like a gentleman, and I won't ask anything else of you.

EVIE. What if I drag you inside and tear your clothes off?

RAUL. That works too.

(pause)

Seven o'clock tonight?

EVIE. I'll see you then.

End of Play